THE ADVENTURES OF SI
ILLUSTRATED AND

CW01622258

BOOK 6

The Man With The Twisted Lip

By Arthur Conan Doyle

Illustrated by Sidney Paget

Annotated by George Cavendish

Solis Press

THE BOOKS IN THIS SERIES

Photo credits: cover and internal images
© Baker Street Scans/Alamy Stock Photo

This edition is based on the complete *Adventures of Sherlock Holmes* published by Solis Press in 2014 (ISBN 978-1-910146-08-8). The individual annotated stories were first published as ebooks in 2011 by Solis Press.

ISBN: 978-1-910146-55-2

Published by Solis Press, Tunbridge Wells, Kent, England

Web: www.solispress.com | *Twitter*: @SolisPress

EDITOR'S INTRODUCTION

The Man With The Twisted Lip is the sixth of Arthur Conan Doyle's 56 short stories that were published in *The Strand Magazine* between 1891 and 1892.

Conan Doyle had introduced Sherlock Holmes, the consulting detective, in his first novel, *A Study in Scarlet* published in 1887, and then again in *The Sign of Four* published in 1890. It might be fair to say that it was not until the serialization of Conan Doyle's stories in *The Strand Magazine* that the public's imagination was caught by the accounts of Sherlock Holmes's cases. Indeed, the magazine was extremely popular at the time: circulation was at around 500,000 copies a month through to the 1930s.

In *The Man With The Twisted Lip*, the sixth of the twelve short stories that make up *The Adventures of Sherlock Holmes*, the narrative is taken up as usual by Dr. John Watson, who was Holmes's friend and confidant. Watson acted as an unofficial biographer, and in the story we read his account of the case.

The character of Watson was introduced in the very first book as a British army doctor who had been discharged from active duty in Afghanistan after suffering a gunshot injury. Watson was searching for a place to live in London and met Sherlock Holmes who too was in need of accommodation. They decided to share the expense of lodging in 221b Baker Street. After living in Baker Street, Watson moved away when he married. In this story he is reminiscing with his old friend.

The text is close to that as first published. I have edited some of the spellings, so that they are the ones more commonly used nowadays, otherwise the text is unaltered.

As the story was written over 120 years ago, I felt that some explanation was needed to help those readers who are not familiar with some of the phrases used by the author and his characters. Some phrases are still in use in modern-day British English, but I have attempted to describe some of these to make the text clearer to English speakers from outside of the UK, or to those who do not speak English as a first language. I have also included some background information on places, names and terms used in the story.

It is not essential to consult the notes when reading this book. However, I hope that my explanations will enhance the reader's enjoyment of this story by giving them some insights that might otherwise have been missed.

George Cavendish

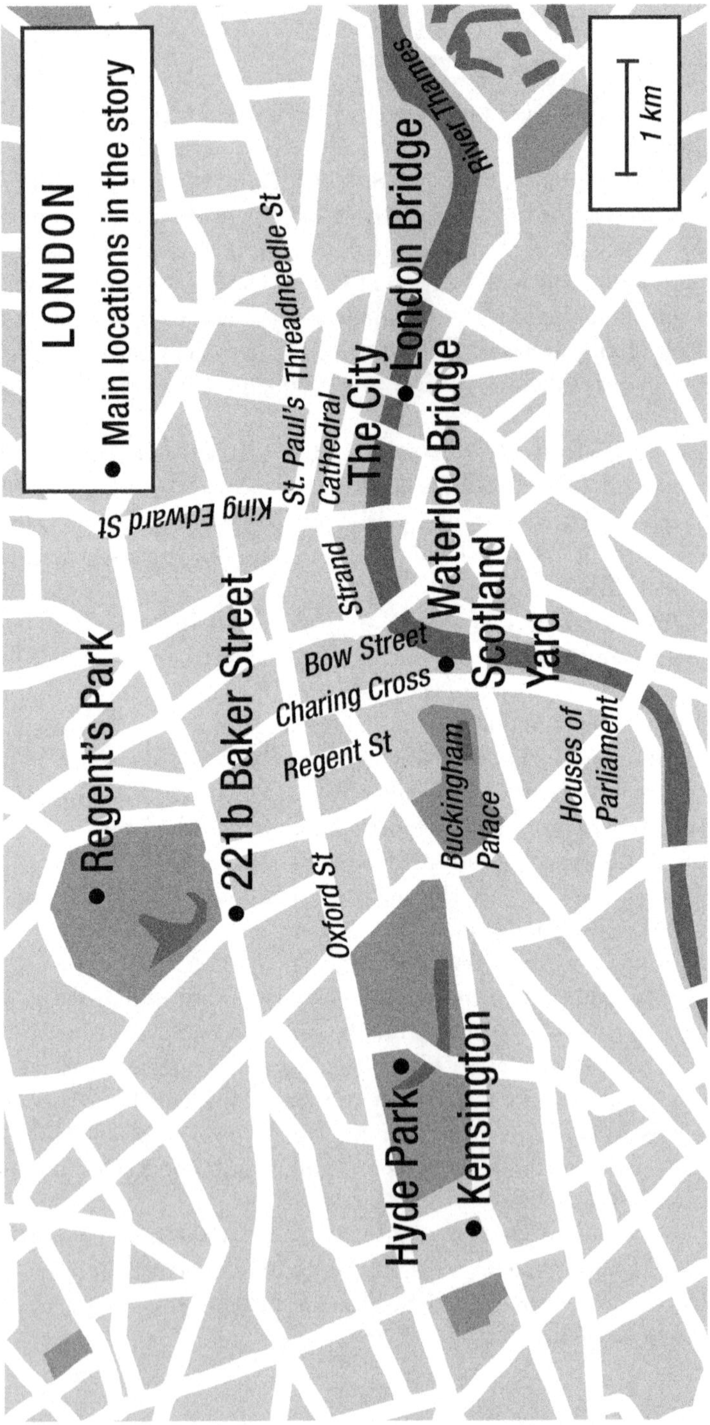
LONDON
Main locations in the story
Regent's Park
221b Baker Street
King Edward St
St. Paul's
Cathedral
Threadneedle St
The City
London Bridge
Waterloo Bridge
Strand
Bow Street
Charing Cross
Scotland
Yard
Regent St
Oxford St
Buckingham
Palace
Houses of
Parliament
Hyde Park
Kensington
River Thames
1 km

THE MAN WITH THE TWISTED LIP

Isa Whitney, brother of the late Elias Whitney, D.D.,[1] Principal of the Theological College of St. George's,[2] was much addicted to opium.[3] The habit grew upon him, as I understand, from some foolish freak when he was at college; for having read De Quincey's description of his dreams and sensations,[4] he had drenched his tobacco with laudanum in an attempt to produce the same effects. He found, as so many more have done, that the practice is easier to attain than to get rid of, and for many years he continued to be a slave to the drug, an object of mingled horror and pity to his friends and relatives. I can see him now, with yellow, pasty face, drooping lids, and pinpoint pupils, all huddled in a chair, the wreck and ruin of a noble man.

One night – it was in June, '89[5] – there came a ring to my bell, about the hour when a man gives his first yawn and glances at the clock. I sat up in my chair, and my wife[6] laid her needlework down in her lap and made a little face of disappointment.

"A patient!" said she. "You'll have to go out."[7]

---

1 Doctor of Divinity (*Divinitatis Doctor* in Latin) is an academic degree in the study of Christian and other theology.

2 A made-up college name.

3 From the opium poppy, it contains a proportion of morphine which is a narcotic drug.

4 Thomas de Quincey (1785–1859) was an English author who wrote *Confessions of an English Opium-Eater* in 1821. It is an autobiographical account about his laudanum (opium and alcohol mixture) addiction and its effect on his life.

5 1889.

6 Watson meets and marries Mary Morstan. (Covered in *The Sign of Four*, published in 1890 and set in 1887 or 1888.)

7 Watson used to be an army doctor and now he was practising as a general practitioner, or family doctor. In *The Red-Headed League*, Watson says that he lives in Kensington, an affluent district in west London, a short distance from his old lodgings in 221b Baker Street.

I groaned, for I was newly come back from a weary day.

We heard the door open, a few hurried words, and then quick steps upon the linoleum.[8] Our own door flew open, and a lady, clad in some dark-coloured stuff, with a black veil, entered the room.

"You will excuse my calling so late," she began, and then, suddenly losing her self-control, she ran forward, threw her arms about my wife's neck, and sobbed upon her shoulder. "Oh, I'm in such trouble!" she cried; "I do so want a little help."

"Why," said my wife, pulling up her veil, "it is Kate Whitney. How you startled me, Kate! I had not an idea who you were when you came in."

"I didn't know what to do, so I came straight to you." That was always the way. Folk who were in grief came to my wife like birds to a lighthouse.

"It was very sweet of you to come. Now, you must have some wine and water, and sit here comfortably and tell us all about it. Or should you rather that I sent John[9] off to bed?"

"Oh, no, no! I want the doctor's advice and help, too. It's about Isa. He has not been home for two days. I am so frightened about him!"

It was not the first time that she had spoken to us of her husband's trouble, to me as a doctor, to my wife as an old friend and school companion. We soothed and comforted her by such words as we could find. Did she know where her husband was? Was it possible that we could bring him back to her?

It seems that it was. She had the surest information that of late he had, when the fit was on him, made use of an opi-

---

8 Commonly called "lino", it was a manufactured floor covering. The first manufacturing company opened in 1864.

9 In the original text this is James. As Watson's first name is John, I've considered this to be an error by the author or a typographical mistake. Many amusing pages have been filled over the years with speculation about this mix up.

um den in the farthest east of the City.[10] Hitherto his orgies had always been confined to one day, and he had come back, twitching and shattered, in the evening. But now the spell had been upon him eight-and-forty hours, and he lay there, doubtless among the dregs of the docks, breathing in the poison or sleeping off the effects. There he was to be found, she was sure of it, at the Bar of Gold, in Upper Swandam Lane.[11] But what was she to do? How could she, a young and timid woman, make her way into such a place and pluck her husband out from among the ruffians who surrounded him?

There was the case, and of course there was but one way out of it. Might I not escort her to this place? And then, as a second thought, why should she come at all? I was Isa Whitney's medical adviser, and as such I had influence over him. I could manage it better if I were alone. I promised her on my word that I would send him home in a cab within two hours if he were indeed at the address which she had given me. And so in ten minutes I had left my armchair and cheery sitting room behind me, and was speeding eastward in a hansom[12] on a strange errand, as it seemed to me at the time, though the future only could show how strange it was to be.

But there was no great difficulty in the first stage of my adventure. Upper Swandam Lane is a vile alley lurking behind the high wharves which line the north side of the river to the east of London Bridge.[13] Between a slop shop[14] and a

---

10 The City of London (with a capital C) is a separate district within London. It is also the financial centre of London. The farthest eastern part would have included the docks on the Thames.

11 A made-up public house name in a fictitious street.

12 In full, a hansom cab – a taxi. It would have been two-wheeled carriage pulled by a single horse. Named after J.A. Hansom, its designer.

13 Not to be confused with the more elaborate Tower Bridge. London Bridge is about 6 miles, 10 km, from Watson's home in Kensington. The present bridge was opened in 1973. The previous bridge was sold to an American company and there were rumours and jokey stories that it thought it was buying the iconic Tower Bridge. This has since been demonstrated to be untrue.

14 An archaic term for a place selling cheap clothing.

gin shop,[15] approached by a steep flight of steps leading down to a black gap like the mouth of a cave, I found the den of which I was in search. Ordering my cab to wait, I passed down the steps, worn hollow in the centre by the ceaseless tread of drunken feet; and by the light of a flickering oil-lamp above the door I found the latch and made my way into a long, low room, thick and heavy with the brown opium smoke, and terraced with wooden berths, like the forecastle[16] of an emigrant ship.

Through the gloom one could dimly catch a glimpse of bodies lying in strange fantastic poses, bowed shoulders, bent knees, heads thrown back, and chins pointing upward, with here and there a dark, lack-lustre eye turned upon the newcomer. Out of the black shadows there glimmered little red circles of light, now bright, now faint, as the burning poison waxed or waned in the bowls of the metal pipes. The most lay silent, but some muttered to themselves, and others talked together in a strange, low, monotonous voice, their conversation coming in gushes, and then suddenly tailing off into silence, each mumbling out his own thoughts and paying little heed to the words of his neighbour. At the farther end was a small brazier of burning charcoal, beside which on a three-legged wooden stool there sat a tall, thin old man, with his jaw resting upon his two fists, and his elbows upon his knees, staring into the fire.

As I entered, a sallow Malay[17] attendant had hurried up with a pipe for me and a supply of the drug, beckoning me to an empty berth.

"Thank you. I have not come to stay," said I. "There is a friend of mine here, Mr. Isa Whitney, and I wish to speak with him."

---

15 Selling gin to take away or to drink standing up.

16 The upper deck of a sailing ship. Usually pronounced fo'c's'le.

17 A native of Malaysia.

STARING INTO THE FIRE.

There was a movement and an exclamation from my right, and peering through the gloom, I saw Whitney, pale, haggard, and unkempt, staring out at me.

"My God! It's Watson," said he. He was in a pitiable state of reaction, with every nerve in a twitter. "I say, Watson, what o'clock is it?"

"Nearly eleven."

"Of what day?"

"Of Friday, June 19th."

"Good heavens! I thought it was Wednesday. It is Wednesday. What d'you want to frighten a chap for?" He sank his face onto his arms and began to sob in a high treble key.

"I tell you that it is Friday,[18] man. Your wife has been waiting this two days for you. You should be ashamed of yourself!"

"So I am. But you've got mixed, Watson, for I have only been here a few hours, three pipes, four pipes – I forget how many. But I'll go home with you. I wouldn't frighten Kate – poor little Kate. Give me your hand! Have you a cab?"

"Yes, I have one waiting."

"Then I shall go in it. But I must owe something. Find what I owe, Watson. I am all off colour. I can do nothing for myself."

I walked down the narrow passage between the double row of sleepers, holding my breath to keep out the vile, stupefying fumes of the drug, and looking about for the manager. As I passed the tall man who sat by the brazier I felt a sudden pluck at my skirt,[19] and a low voice whispered, "Walk past me, and then look back at me." The words fell quite distinctly upon my ear. I glanced down. They could only have come from the old man at my side, and yet he sat now as absorbed as ever, very thin, very wrinkled, bent with age, an opium pipe dangling down from between his knees, as though it had dropped in sheer lassitude from his fingers. I took two steps forward and looked back. It took all my self-control to prevent me from breaking out into a cry of astonishment. He had turned his back so that none could see him but I. His form had filled out, his wrinkles were gone, the dull eyes had regained their fire, and there, sitting by the fire and grinning at my surprise, was none other than Sherlock Holmes. He made a slight motion to me to approach him, and instantly,

18 June 19th, 1889 *was* actually a Wednesday!
19 The skirt of his long-skirted jacket.

"HOLMES!" I WHISPERED.

as he turned his face half round to the company once more, subsided into a doddering, loose-lipped senility.[20]

"Holmes!" I whispered, "what on earth are you doing in this den?"

"As low as you can," he answered; "I have excellent ears. If you would have the great kindness to get rid of that sottish[21] friend of yours I should be exceedingly glad to have a little talk with you."

"I have a cab outside."

20 Weakness of old age.
21 Drunk.

"Then pray send him home in it. You may safely trust him, for he appears to be too limp to get into any mischief. I should recommend you also to send a note by the cabman to your wife to say that you have thrown in your lot with me. If you will wait outside, I shall be with you in five minutes."

It was difficult to refuse any of Sherlock Holmes's requests, for they were always so exceedingly definite, and put forward with such a quiet air of mastery. I felt, however, that when Whitney was once confined in the cab my mission was practically accomplished; and for the rest, I could not wish anything better than to be associated with my friend in one of those singular adventures which were the normal condition of his existence. In a few minutes I had written my note, paid Whitney's bill, led him out to the cab, and seen him driven through the darkness. In a very short time a decrepit figure had emerged from the opium den, and I was walking down the street with Sherlock Holmes. For two streets he shuffled along with a bent back and an uncertain foot. Then, glancing quickly round, he straightened himself out and burst into a hearty fit of laughter.

"I suppose, Watson," said he, "that you imagine that I have added opium-smoking to cocaine injections, and all the other little weaknesses on which you have favoured me with your medical views."[22]

"I was certainly surprised to find you there."

"But not more so than I to find you."

"I came to find a friend."

"And I to find an enemy."

"An enemy?"

"Yes; one of my natural enemies, or, shall I say, my natural prey. Briefly, Watson, I am in the midst of a very remarkable inquiry, and I have hoped to find a clue in the incoher-

---

22 Cocaine was not a controlled drug in the UK until 1916, when it was outlawed by emergency legislation introduced at the time of the First World War (1914–18).

ent ramblings of these sots, as I have done before now. Had I been recognized in that den my life would not have been worth an hour's purchase; for I have used it before now for my own purposes, and the rascally Lascar[23] who runs it has sworn to have vengeance upon me. There is a trapdoor at the back of that building, near the corner of Paul's Wharf, which could tell some strange tales of what has passed through it upon the moonless nights."

"What! You do not mean bodies?"

"Ay,[24] bodies, Watson. We should be rich men if we had £1000 for every poor devil who has been done to death in that den. It is the vilest murder-trap on the whole riverside, and I fear that Neville St. Clair has entered it never to leave it more. But our trap should be here." He put his two fore-fingers between his teeth and whistled shrilly – a signal which was answered by a similar whistle from the distance, followed shortly by the rattle of wheels and the clink of horses' hoofs.

"Now, Watson," said Holmes, as a tall dogcart[25] dashed up through the gloom, throwing out two golden tunnels of yellow light from its side lanterns. "You'll come with me, won't you?"

"If I can be of use."

"Oh, a trusty comrade is always of use; and a chronicler still more so. My room at The Cedars is a double-bedded one."

"The Cedars?"

"Yes; that is Mr. St. Clair's house. I am staying there while I conduct the inquiry."

"Where is it, then?"

"Near Lee, in Kent.[26] We have a seven-mile drive[27] before us."

23 An Indian seaman.
24 Normally "aye"; an archaic version of yes.
25 A type of two-wheeled cart drawn by a single horse.
26 Now part of the London Borough of Lewisham in south London.
27 About 11 km.

"But I am all in the dark."

"Of course you are. You'll know all about it presently. Jump up here. All right, John; we shall not need you. Here's half a crown.[28] Look out for me tomorrow, about eleven. Give her her head.[29] So long, then!"

He flicked the horse with his whip, and we dashed away through the endless succession of sombre and deserted streets, which widened gradually, until we were flying across a broad balustraded[30] bridge,[31] with the murky river flowing sluggishly beneath us. Beyond lay another dull wilderness of bricks and mortar, its silence broken only by the heavy, regular footfall of the policeman, or the songs and shouts of some belated party of revellers. A dull rack[32] was drifting slowly across the sky, and a star or two twinkled dimly here and there through the rifts of the clouds. Holmes drove in silence, with his head sunk upon his breast, and the air of a man who is lost in thought, while I sat beside him, curious to learn what this new quest might be which seemed to tax his powers so sorely, and yet afraid to break in upon the current of his thoughts. We had driven several miles, and were beginning to get to the fringe of the belt of suburban villas,[33] when he shook himself, shrugged his shoulders, and lit up his pipe with the air of a man who has satisfied himself that he is acting for the best.

"You have a grand gift of silence, Watson," said he. "It makes you quite invaluable as a companion. 'Pon[34] my word, it is a great thing for me to have someone to talk to, for my

---

28 A coin of the value of 2 shillings and 6 pence; that is 12.5 pence in modern money.

29 Loosening a horse's reins and letting it go at its own speed.

30 Balustrades are railings supported by short posts.

31 Presumably this is London Bridge as it is the only bridge on their route to Lee, and Watson describes Upper Swandam Lane as being north of the Thames.

32 Driving clouds.

33 Small and elegant detached houses.

34 A contraction of upon.

HE FLICKED THE HORSE WITH HIS WHIP.

own thoughts are not over-pleasant. I was wondering what I should say to this dear little woman tonight when she meets me at the door."

"You forget that I know nothing about it."

"I shall just have time to tell you the facts of the case before we get to Lee. It seems absurdly simple, and yet, somehow I can get nothing to go upon. There's plenty of thread, no doubt, but I can't get the end of it into my hand. Now,

I'll state the case clearly and concisely to you, Watson, and maybe you can see a spark where all is dark to me."

"Proceed, then."

"Some years ago – to be definite, in May, 1884 – there came to Lee a gentleman, Neville St. Clair by name, who appeared to have plenty of money. He took a large villa, laid out the grounds very nicely, and lived generally in good style. By degrees he made friends in the neighbourhood, and in 1887 he married the daughter of a local brewer, by whom he now has two children. He had no occupation, but was interested in several companies and went into town as a rule in the morning, returning by the 5:14 from Cannon Street[35] every night. Mr. St. Clair is now thirty-seven years of age, is a man of temperate[36] habits, a good husband, a very affectionate father, and a man who is popular with all who know him. I may add that his whole debts at the present moment, as far as we have been able to ascertain, amount to £88 10*s.*,[37] while he has £220[38] standing to his credit in the Capital and Counties Bank.[39] There is no reason, therefore, to think that money troubles have been weighing upon his mind.

"Last Monday Mr. Neville St. Clair went into town[40] rather earlier than usual, remarking before he started that he had two important commissions to perform, and that he would bring his little boy home a box of bricks.[41] Now, by the merest chance, his wife received a telegram upon this same Monday, very shortly after his departure, to the effect that a small parcel of considerable value which she had been expecting was waiting for her at the offices of the Aberdeen Shipping

35 A train station in the City of London.
36 Moderate, avoiding excess.
37 £88.50 in modern money. The *s.* indicates shillings, of which there were 20 to a pound. A *d.* represents pennies of which there were 12 to a shilling.
38 Equivalent to about £13,000 today.
39 A real bank whose name disappeared as the result of a merger in 1918.
40 To go into town was to travel into London.
41 Toy building blocks.

Company. Now, if you are well up in your London, you will know that the office of the company is in Fresno Street,[42] which branches out of Upper Swandam Lane, where you found me tonight. Mrs. St. Clair had her lunch, started for the City, did some shopping, proceeded to the company's office, got her packet, and found herself at exactly 4:35 walking through Swandam Lane on her way back to the station. Have you followed me so far?"

"It is very clear."

"If you remember, Monday was an exceedingly hot day, and Mrs. St. Clair walked slowly, glancing about in the hope of seeing a cab, as she did not like the neighbourhood in which she found herself. While she was walking in this way down Swandam Lane, she suddenly heard an ejaculation or cry, and was struck cold to see her husband looking down at her and, as it seemed to her, beckoning to her from a second-floor window. The window was open, and she distinctly saw his face, which she describes as being terribly agitated. He waved his hands frantically to her, and then vanished from the window so suddenly that it seemed to her that he had been plucked back by some irresistible force from behind. One singular point which struck her quick feminine eye was that although he wore some dark coat, such as he had started to town in, he had on neither collar[43] nor necktie.

"Convinced that something was amiss with him, she rushed down the steps – for the house was none other than the opium den in which you found me tonight – and running through the front room she attempted to ascend the stairs which led to the first floor. At the foot of the stairs, however, she met this Lascar scoundrel of whom I have spoken, who thrust her back and, aided by a Dane, who acts as assistant there, pushed her out into the street. Filled with the most maddening doubts

42 A made-up company and made-up street name.

43 Shirt collars were often removable at the time.

AT THE FOOT OF THE STAIRS, HOWEVER, SHE MET THIS LASCAR SCOUNDREL.

and fears, she rushed down the lane and, by rare good fortune, met in Fresno Street a number of constables with an inspector,[44] all on their way to their beat.[45] The inspector and two men accompanied her back, and in spite of the continued resistance of the proprietor, they made their way to the room in which Mr. St. Clair had last been seen. There was no sign of him there. In fact, in the whole of that floor there was no one to be found save a crippled wretch of hideous aspect, who, it seems, made his home there. Both he and the Lascar stoutly swore that no one else had been in the front room during the afternoon. So determined was their denial that the inspector was staggered, and had almost come to believe that Mrs. St. Clair had been deluded when, with a cry, she sprang at a small deal box[46] which lay upon the table and tore the lid from it. Out there fell a cascade of children's bricks. It was the toy which he had promised to bring home.

"This discovery, and the evident confusion which the cripple showed, made the inspector realize that the matter was serious. The rooms were carefully examined, and results all pointed to an abominable crime. The front room was plainly furnished as a sitting room and led into a small bedroom, which looked out upon the back of one of the wharves. Between the wharf and the bedroom window is a narrow strip, which is dry at low tide but is covered at high tide with at least four and a half feet[47] of water. The bedroom window was a broad one and opened from below. On examination traces of blood were to be seen upon the windowsill, and several scattered drops were visible upon the wooden floor of the bedroom. Thrust away behind a curtain in the front room were all the clothes of Mr. Neville St. Clair, with the exception of his coat. His boots, his socks, his hat, and his watch – all

44 Police constables and an inspector of police.
45 A beat is an area patrolled by police officers.
46 A box made of strips of wood.
47 Over 1 metre.

were there. There were no signs of violence upon any of these garments, and there were no other traces of Mr. Neville St. Clair. Out of the window he must apparently have gone for no other exit could be discovered, and the ominous bloodstains upon the sill gave little promise that he could save himself by swimming, for the tide was at its very highest at the moment of the tragedy.

"And now as to the villains who seemed to be immediately implicated in the matter. The Lascar was known to be a man of the vilest antecedents, but as, by Mrs. St. Clair's story, he was known to have been at the foot of the stair within a very few seconds of her husband's appearance at the window, he could hardly have been more than an accessory to the crime. His defence was one of absolute ignorance, and he protested that he had no knowledge as to the doings of Hugh Boone, his lodger, and that he could not account in any way for the presence of the missing gentleman's clothes.

"So much for the Lascar manager. Now for the sinister cripple who lives upon the second floor of the opium den, and who was certainly the last human being whose eyes rested upon Neville St. Clair. His name is Hugh Boone, and his hideous face is one which is familiar to every man who goes much to the City. He is a professional beggar, though in order to avoid the police regulations he pretends to a small trade in wax vestas.[48] Some little distance down Threadneedle Street,[49] upon the left-hand side, there is, as you may have remarked, a small angle in the wall. Here it is that this creature takes his daily seat, cross-legged with his tiny stock of matches on his lap, and as he is a piteous spectacle a small rain of charity descends into the greasy leather cap which lies upon the pave-

48 A type of match for lighting fires and so on.

49 A major street in the commercial part of London known as the City. The City of London (with a capital C) is a separate district within London. The Bank of England (nicknamed "The Old Lady of Threadneedle Street") has been situated there since 1734.

HE IS A PROFESSIONAL BEGGAR.

ment beside him. I have watched the fellow more than once before ever I thought of making his professional acquaintance, and I have been surprised at the harvest which he has reaped in a short time. His appearance, you see, is so remarkable that no one can pass him without observing him. A shock of orange hair, a pale face disfigured by a horrible scar, which, by its contraction, has turned up the outer edge of his upper lip, a bulldog chin, and a pair of very penetrating dark eyes, which present a singular contrast to the colour of his hair, all mark him out from amid the common crowd of mendicants[50] and so, too, does his wit, for he is ever ready with a reply to any piece of chaff[51] which may be thrown at him by the passers-by. This is the man whom we now learn to have been the lodger at the opium den, and to have been the last man to see the gentleman of whom we are in quest."

"But a cripple!" said I. "What could he have done single-handed against a man in the prime of life?"

"He is a cripple in the sense that he walks with a limp; but in other respects he appears to be a powerful and well-nurtured man. Surely your medical experience would tell you, Watson, that weakness in one limb is often compensated for by exceptional strength in the others."

"Pray continue your narrative."

"Mrs. St. Clair had fainted at the sight of the blood upon the window, and she was escorted home in a cab by the police, as her presence could be of no help to them in their investigations. Inspector Barton, who had charge of the case, made a very careful examination of the premises, but without finding anything which threw any light upon the matter. One mistake had been made in not arresting Boone instantly, as he was allowed some few minutes during which he might have communicated with his friend the Lascar, but this fault was soon remedied, and he was seized and searched, without anything being found which could incriminate him. There were, it is true, some blood stains upon his right shirt sleeve, but he pointed to his ring-finger, which had been cut near the nail, and explained that the bleeding came from there, adding that he had been to the window not long before, and that the stains which had been observed there came doubtless from the same

50 Another word for beggars.

51 Banter or light-hearted joking.

source. He denied strenuously having ever seen Mr. Neville St. Clair and swore that the presence of the clothes in his room was as much a mystery to him as to the police. As to Mrs. St. Clair's assertion that she had actually seen her husband at the window, he declared that she must have been either mad or dreaming. He was removed, loudly protesting, to the police station, while the inspector remained upon the premises in the hope that the ebbing tide might afford some fresh clue.

"And it did, though they hardly found upon the mud-bank what they had feared to find. It was Neville St. Clair's coat, and not Neville St. Clair, which lay uncovered as the tide receded. And what do you think they found in the pockets?"

"I cannot imagine."

"No, I don't think you would guess. Every pocket stuffed with pennies and half-pennies – 421 pennies and 270 half-pennies.[52] It was no wonder that it had not been swept away by the tide. But a human body is a different matter. There is a fierce eddy between the wharf and the house. It seemed likely enough that the weighted coat had remained when the stripped body had been sucked away into the river."

"But I understand that all the other clothes were found in the room. Would the body be dressed in a coat alone?"

"No, sir, but the facts might be met speciously enough. Suppose that this man Boone had thrust Neville St. Clair through the window, there is no human eye which could have seen the deed. What would he do then? It would of course instantly strike him that he must get rid of the telltale garments. He would seize the coat, then, and be in the act of throwing it out, when it would occur to him that it would swim and not sink. He has little time, for he has heard the scuffle downstairs when the wife tried to force her way up, and per-

52 £2 6*s*. 4*d*. – about £2.31 in modern money but worth today about £140.

STUFFS ALL THE COINS INTO THE POCKETS.

haps he has already heard from his Lascar confederate[53] that the police are hurrying up the street. There is not an instant to be lost. He rushes to some secret hoard, where he has accu-

53 Ally or supporter.

mulated the fruits of his beggary, and he stuffs all the coins upon which he can lay his hands into the pockets to make sure of the coat's sinking. He throws it out, and would have done the same with the other garments had not he heard the rush of steps below, and only just had time to close the window when the police appeared."

"It certainly sounds feasible."

"Well, we will take it as a working hypothesis for want of a better. Boone, as I have told you, was arrested and taken to the station, but it could not be shown that there had ever before been anything against him. He had for years been known as a professional beggar, but his life appeared to have been a very quiet and innocent one. There the matter stands at present, and the questions which have to be solved – what Neville St. Clair was doing in the opium den, what happened to him when there, where is he now, and what Hugh Boone had to do with his disappearance – are all as far from a solution as ever. I confess that I cannot recall any case within my experience which looked at the first glance so simple and yet which presented such difficulties."

While Sherlock Holmes had been detailing this singular series of events, we had been whirling through the outskirts of the great town until the last straggling houses had been left behind, and we rattled along with a country hedge upon either side of us. Just as he finished, however, we drove through two scattered villages, where a few lights still glimmered in the windows.

"We are on the outskirts of Lee," said my companion. "We have touched on three English counties in our short drive, starting in Middlesex, passing over an angle of Surrey, and ending in Kent. See that light among the trees? That is The Cedars, and beside that lamp sits a woman whose anxious ears have already, I have little doubt, caught the clink of our horse's feet."

"But why are you not conducting the case from Baker Street?"[54] I asked.

"Because there are many inquiries which must be made out here. Mrs. St. Clair has most kindly put two rooms at my disposal, and you may rest assured that she will have nothing but a welcome for my friend and colleague. I hate to meet her, Watson, when I have no news of her husband. Here we are. Whoa,[55] there, whoa!"

We had pulled up in front of a large villa which stood within its own grounds. A stable-boy had run out to the horse's head, and springing down, I followed Holmes up the small, winding gravel-drive which led to the house. As we approached, the door flew open, and a little blonde woman stood in the opening, clad in some sort of light mousseline de soie,[56] with a touch of fluffy pink chiffon[57] at her neck and wrists. She stood with her figure outlined against the flood of light, one hand upon the door, one half-raised in her eagerness, her body slightly bent, her head and face protruded, with eager eyes and parted lips, a standing question.

"Well?" she cried, "well?" And then, seeing that there were two of us, she gave a cry of hope which sank into a groan as she saw that my companion shook his head and shrugged his shoulders.

"No good news?"

"None."

---

54 Baker Street was a residential area in central London. The houses were terraced – that is built with shared walls – and made of brick. The address is 221b Baker Street. This didn't exist when the story was written, but the address was assigned in 1990 and houses the Sherlock Holmes Museum. There is no 221a: the "b" represents *bis*, the Latin for "twice". Holmes lived in a rented apartment attached or converted from 221. This would probably have been owned by Mrs. Hudson, Holmes's long-suffering landlady and cook.

55 A command to stop, especially to a horse.

56 A fine crisp fabric made of silk; from the French words for "muslin-like fabric of silk".

57 An ornamental accessory such as a ribbon or lace.

"No bad?"

"No."

"Thank God for that. But come in. You must be weary, for you have had a long day."

"This is my friend, Dr. Watson. He has been of most vital use to me in several of my cases, and a lucky chance has made it possible for me to bring him out and associate him with this investigation."

"I am delighted to see you," said she, pressing my hand warmly. "You will, I am sure, forgive anything that may be wanting in our arrangements, when you consider the blow which has come so suddenly upon us."

"My dear madam," said I, "I am an old campaigner, and if I were not I can very well see that no apology is needed. If I can be of any assistance, either to you or to my friend here, I shall be indeed happy."

"Now, Mr. Sherlock Holmes," said the lady as we entered a well-lit dining-room, upon the table of which a cold supper had been laid out, "I should very much like to ask you one or two plain questions, to which I beg that you will give a plain answer."

"Certainly, madam."

"Do not trouble about my feelings. I am not hysterical, nor given to fainting. I simply wish to hear your real, real opinion."

"Upon what point?"

"In your heart of hearts, do you think that Neville is alive?"

Sherlock Holmes seemed to be embarrassed by the question. "Frankly, now!" she repeated, standing upon the rug and looking keenly down at him as he leaned back in a basket-chair.[58]

"Frankly, then, madam, I do not."

"You think that he is dead?"

58 A wicker chair with arms that are a forward continuation of the back.

"FRANKLY, NOW," SHE REPEATED.

"I do."

"Murdered?"

"I don't say that. Perhaps."

"And on what day did he meet his death?"

"On Monday."

"Then perhaps, Mr. Holmes, you will be good enough to explain how it is that I have received a letter from him today."

Sherlock Holmes sprang out of his chair as if he had been galvanized.[59]

"What!" he roared.

"Yes, today." She stood smiling, holding up a little slip of paper in the air.

"May I see it?"

59 Roused forcibly.

"Certainly."

He snatched it from her in his eagerness, and smoothing it out upon the table he drew over the lamp and examined it intently. I had left my chair and was gazing at it over his shoulder. The envelope was a very coarse one and was stamped with the Gravesend[60] postmark and with the date of that very day, or rather of the day before, for it was considerably after midnight.

"Coarse writing," murmured Holmes. "Surely this is not your husband's writing, madam."

"No, but the enclosure is."

"I perceive also that whoever addressed the envelope had to go and inquire as to the address."

"How can you tell that?"

"The name, you see, is in perfectly black ink, which has dried itself. The rest is of the greyish colour, which shows that blotting-paper[61] has been used. If it had been written straight off, and then blotted, none would be of a deep black shade. This man has written the name, and there has then been a pause before he wrote the address, which can only mean that he was not familiar with it. It is, of course, a trifle,[62] but there is nothing so important as trifles. Let us now see the letter. Ha! there has been an enclosure here!"

"Yes, there was a ring. His signet-ring."[63]

"And you are sure that this is your husband's hand?"

"One of his hands."

"One?"

"His hand when he wrote hurriedly. It is very unlike his usual writing, and yet I know it well."

---

60 A town in Kent along the southern bank of the Thames about 20 miles or 32 km from London Bridge.

61 This would have been used to soak up the excess liquid ink from pens of the time.

62 In this sense something of slight value or importance.

63 A ring with seal set into it. A seal was often a coat of arms that was then used to make an impression in molten wax on the sealing of an envelope.

"'Dearest do not be frightened. All will come well. There is a huge error which it may take some little time to rectify. Wait in patience. – Neville.' Written in pencil upon the fly-leaf[64] of a book, octavo size,[65] no watermark.[66] Hum! Posted today in Gravesend by a man with a dirty thumb. Ha! And the flap has been gummed, if I am not very much in error, by a person who had been chewing tobacco.[67] And you have no doubt that it is your husband's hand, madam?"

"None. Neville wrote those words."

"And they were posted today at Gravesend. Well, Mrs. St. Clair, the clouds lighten, though I should not venture to say that the danger is over."

"But he must be alive, Mr. Holmes."

"Unless this is a clever forgery to put us on the wrong scent. The ring, after all, proves nothing. It may have been taken from him."

"No, no; it is, it is his very own writing!"

"Very well. It may, however, have been written on Monday and only posted today."

"That is possible."

"If so, much may have happened between."

"Oh, you must not discourage me, Mr. Holmes. I know that all is well with him. There is so keen a sympathy between us that I should know if evil came upon him. On the very day that I saw him last he cut himself in the bedroom, and yet I in the dining room rushed upstairs instantly with the utmost certainty that something had happened. Do you think that

64 Also called endpapers. The part of a hardback book that is attached to the hard cover.

65 A size of book. It refers to the size of page obtained from printing 16 pages of text on full sheets of paper, which were then folded three times to produce eight leaves (octavo is derived from the Latin for eight).

66 A faint image in notepaper that is visible when holding the paper to the light. Most often seen in banknotes nowadays.

67 A type of tobacco that is chewed to release its flavour and nicotine.

I would respond to such a trifle and yet be ignorant of his death?"

"I have seen too much not to know that the impression of a woman may be more valuable than the conclusion of an analytical reasoner. And in this letter you certainly have a very strong piece of evidence to corroborate your view. But if your husband is alive and able to write letters, why should he remain away from you?"

"I cannot imagine. It is unthinkable."

"And on Monday he made no remarks before leaving you?"

"No."

"And you were surprised to see him in Swandam Lane?"

"Very much so."

"Was the window open?"

"Yes."

"Then he might have called to you?"

"He might."

"He only, as I understand, gave an inarticulate cry?"

"Yes."

"A call for help, you thought?"

"Yes. He waved his hands."

"But it might have been a cry of surprise. Astonishment at the unexpected sight of you might cause him to throw up his hands?"

"It is possible."

"And you thought he was pulled back?"

"He disappeared so suddenly."

"He might have leaped back. You did not see anyone else in the room?"

"No, but this horrible man confessed to having been there, and the Lascar was at the foot of the stairs."

"Quite so. Your husband, as far as you could see, had his ordinary clothes on?"

"But without his collar or tie. I distinctly saw his bare throat."

"Had he ever spoken of Swandam Lane?"

"Never."

"Had he ever showed any signs of having taken opium?"

"Never."

"Thank you, Mrs. St. Clair. Those are the principal points about which I wished to be absolutely clear. We shall now have a little supper and then retire, for we may have a very busy day tomorrow."

A large and comfortable double-bedded room had been placed at our disposal, and I was quickly between the sheets, for I was weary after my night of adventure. Sherlock Holmes was a man, however, who, when he had an unsolved problem upon his mind, would go for days, and even for a week, without rest, turning it over, rearranging his facts, looking at it from every point of view until he had either fathomed it or convinced himself that his data were insufficient. It was soon evident to me that he was now preparing for an all-night sitting. He took off his coat and waistcoat, put on a large blue dressing-gown, and then wandered about the room collecting pillows from his bed and cushions from the sofa and armchairs. With these he constructed a sort of Eastern divan,[68] upon which he perched himself cross-legged, with an ounce of shag tobacco[69] and a box of matches laid out in front of him. In the dim light of the lamp I saw him sitting there, an old briar pipe[70] between his lips, his eyes fixed vacantly upon the corner of the ceiling, the blue smoke curling up from him, silent, motionless, with the light shining upon his strong-set aquiline[71] features. So he sat as I dropped off to sleep, and so he sat when a sudden ejaculation[72] caused me to wake up,

68 A type of padded seat set against a wall.

69 Rolling tobacco used to make cigarettes, it would have been thought of as low quality.

70 A pipe made from the root of the *Erica arborea* tree.

71 From "eagle-like" – he had a big nose.

72 Sudden utterance.

THE PIPE WAS STILL BETWEEN HIS LIPS.

and I found the summer sun shining into the apartment. The pipe was still between his lips, the smoke still curled upward, and the room was full of a dense tobacco haze, but nothing remained of the heap of shag which I had seen upon the previous night.

"Awake, Watson?" he asked.

"Yes."

"Game for a morning drive?"

"Certainly."

"Then dress. No one is stirring yet, but I know where the stable-boy sleeps, and we shall soon have the trap[73] out." He chuckled to himself as he spoke, his eyes twinkled, and he seemed a different man to the sombre thinker of the previous night.

As I dressed I glanced at my watch. It was no wonder that no one was stirring. It was twenty-five minutes past four. I had hardly finished when Holmes returned with the news that the boy was putting in the horse.

"I want to test a little theory of mine," said he, pulling on his boots. "I think, Watson, that you are now standing in the presence of one of the most absolute fools in Europe. I deserve to be kicked from here to Charing Cross.[74] But I think I have the key of the affair now."

"And where is it?" I asked, smiling.

"In the bathroom," he answered. "Oh, yes, I am not joking," he continued, seeing my look of incredulity. "I have just been there, and I have taken it out, and I have got it in this Gladstone bag.[75] Come on, my boy, and we shall see whether it will not fit the lock."

We made our way downstairs as quietly as possible, and out into the bright morning sunshine. In the road stood our horse and trap, with the half-clad stable-boy waiting at the head. We both sprang in, and away we dashed down the London Road. A few country carts were stirring, bearing in vegetables to the metropolis,[76] but the lines of villas on either side were as silent and lifeless as some city in a dream.

"It has been in some points a singular case," said Holmes, flicking the horse on into a gallop. "I confess that I have been

---

73 A horse-drawn two-wheeled carriage.

74 A central London train station with connections to stations in Kent.

75 A bag like a hinged briefcase. Named after William Ewart Gladstone (1809–98), a British politician.

76 The capital city.

as blind as a mole,[77] but it is better to learn wisdom late than never to learn it at all."

In town the earliest risers were just beginning to look sleepily from their windows as we drove through the streets of the Surrey side. Passing down the Waterloo Bridge Road we crossed over the river, and dashing up Wellington Street wheeled sharply to the right and found ourselves in Bow Street.[78] Sherlock Holmes was well known to the force, and the two constables at the door saluted him. One of them held the horse's head while the other led us in.

"Who is on duty?" asked Holmes.

"Inspector Bradstreet, sir."

"Ah, Bradstreet, how are you?" A tall, stout official had come down the stone-flagged passage, in a peaked cap and frogged jacket.[79] "I wish to have a quiet word with you, Bradstreet." "Certainly, Mr. Holmes. Step into my room here." It was a small, office-like room, with a huge ledger upon the table, and a telephone projecting from the wall. The inspector sat down at his desk.

"What can I do for you, Mr. Holmes?"

"I called about that beggarman, Boone – the one who was charged with being concerned in the disappearance of Mr. Neville St. Clair, of Lee."

"Yes. He was brought up and remanded for further inquiries."

"So I heard. You have him here?"

"In the cells."

"Is he quiet?"

"Oh, he gives no trouble. But he is a dirty scoundrel."

"Dirty?"

---

77 Moles are supposed to have poor eyesight as they live in the dark.

78 A street in the Covent Garden area of London, which at the time had a police station. It was also in Bow Street that London's first professional police force was based, the Bow Street Runners.

79 A jacket that has ornamental loops along the front for fastening buttons.

"Yes, it is all we can do to make him wash his hands, and his face is as black as a tinker's. Well, when once his case has been settled, he will have a regular prison bath; and I think, if you saw him, you would agree with me that he needed it."

"I should like to see him very much."

"Would you? That is easily done. Come this way. You can leave your bag."

"No, I think that I'll take it."

"Very good. Come this way, if you please." He led us down a passage, opened a barred door, passed down a winding stair, and brought us to a whitewashed corridor with a line of doors on each side.

"The third on the right is his," said the inspector. "Here it is!" He quietly shot back a panel in the upper part of the door and glanced through.

"He is asleep," said he. "You can see him very well."

We both put our eyes to the grating. The prisoner lay with his face towards us, in a very deep sleep, breathing slowly and heavily. He was a middle-sized man, coarsely clad as became his calling, with a coloured shirt protruding through the rent[80] in his tattered coat. He was, as the inspector had said, extremely dirty, but the grime which covered his face could not conceal its repulsive ugliness. A broad wheal[81] from an old scar ran right across it from eye to chin, and by its contraction had turned up one side of the upper lip, so that three teeth were exposed in a perpetual snarl. A shock of very bright red hair grew low over his eyes and forehead.

"He's a beauty, isn't he?" said the inspector.

"He certainly needs a wash," remarked Holmes. "I had an idea that he might, and I took the liberty of bringing the tools with me." He opened the Gladstone bag as he spoke, and took out, to my astonishment, a very large bath sponge.

---

80 A tear or opening.

81 Or weal; a ridge on the skin as a result of an injury.

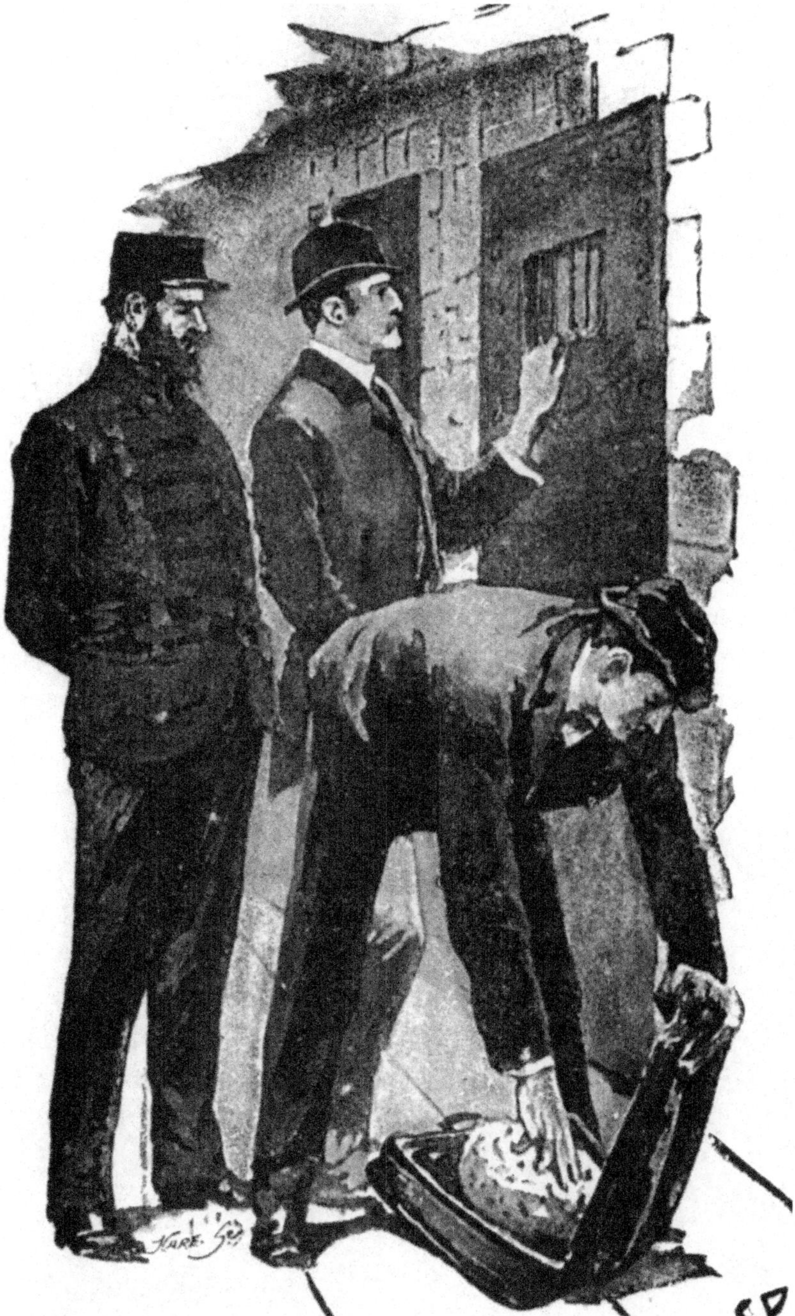

HE TOOK OUT A VERY LARGE BATH SPONGE.

"He! he! You are a funny one," chuckled the inspector.

"Now, if you will have the great goodness to open that door very quietly, we will soon make him cut a much more respectable figure."

"Well, I don't know why not," said the inspector. "He doesn't look a credit to the Bow Street cells, does he?" He slipped his key into the lock, and we all very quietly entered the cell. The sleeper half turned, and then settled down once more into a deep slumber. Holmes stooped to the water-jug, moistened his sponge, and then rubbed it twice vigorously across and down the prisoner's face.

"Let me introduce you," he shouted, "to Mr. Neville St. Clair, of Lee, in the county of Kent."

Never in my life have I seen such a sight. The man's face peeled off under the sponge like the bark from a tree. Gone was the coarse brown tint! Gone, too, was the horrid scar which had seamed it across, and the twisted lip which had given the repulsive sneer to the face! A twitch brought away the tangled red hair, and there, sitting up in his bed,

HE BROKE INTO A SCREAM.

was a pale, sad-faced, refined-looking man, black-haired and smooth-skinned, rubbing his eyes and staring about him with sleepy bewilderment. Then suddenly realizing the exposure, he broke into a scream and threw himself down with his face to the pillow.

"Great heavens!" cried the inspector, "it is, indeed, the missing man. I know him from the photograph."

The prisoner turned with the reckless air of a man who abandons himself to his destiny. "Be it so," said he. "And pray what am I charged with?"

"With making away with Mr. Neville St. – Oh, come, you can't be charged with that unless they make a case of attempted suicide of it," said the inspector with a grin. "Well, I have been twenty-seven years in the force, but this really takes the cake."[82]

"If I am Mr. Neville St. Clair, then it is obvious that no crime has been committed, and that, therefore, I am illegally detained."

"No crime, but a very great error has been committed," said Holmes. "You would have done better to have trusted your wife."

"It was not the wife; it was the children," groaned the prisoner. "God help me, I would not have them ashamed of their father. My God! What an exposure! What can I do?"

Sherlock Holmes sat down beside him on the couch and patted him kindly on the shoulder.

"If you leave it to a court of law to clear the matter up," said he, "of course you can hardly avoid publicity. On the other hand, if you convince the police authorities that there is no possible case against you, I do not know that there is any reason that the details should find their way into the papers. Inspector Bradstreet would, I am sure, make notes upon

82 To take the cake (or biscuit more commonly nowadays) is something in the most extreme case.

anything which you might tell us and submit it to the proper authorities. The case would then never go into court at all."

"God bless you!" cried the prisoner passionately. "I would have endured imprisonment, ay, even execution, rather than have left my miserable secret as a family blot to my children.

"You are the first who have ever heard my story. My father was a schoolmaster in Chesterfield,[83] where I received an excellent education. I travelled in my youth, took to the stage, and finally became a reporter on an evening paper in London. One day my editor wished to have a series of articles upon begging in the metropolis, and I volunteered to supply them. There was the point from which all my adventures started. It was only by trying begging as an amateur that I could get the facts upon which to base my articles. When an actor I had, of course, learned all the secrets of making up, and had been famous in the green-room[84] for my skill. I took advantage now of my attainments. I painted my face, and to make myself as pitiable[85] as possible I made a good scar and fixed one side of my lip in a twist by the aid of a small slip of flesh-coloured plaster. Then with a red head of hair, and an appropriate dress, I took my station in the business part of the city, ostensibly as a match-seller but really as a beggar. For seven hours I plied my trade, and when I returned home in the evening I found to my surprise that I had received no less than twenty-six shillings and fourpence.[86]

"I wrote my articles and thought little more of the matter until, some time later, I backed a bill for a friend and had a writ[87] served upon me for £25.[88] I was at my wit's end where to get the money, but a sudden idea came to me. I begged a fort-

83 A market town 150 miles or 240 km north of London.
84 The room in a theatre in which actors gather when not performing.
85 Deserving of pity.
86 The equivalent of about £1.32 in modern money, the equivalent of about £80 today. A builder at the time would have earned about 30p.
87 A court order.
88 The equivalent today of about £1500.

night's grace from the creditor, asked for a holiday from my employers, and spent the time in begging in the City under my disguise. In ten days I had the money and had paid the debt.

"Well, you can imagine how hard it was to settle down to arduous work at £2 a week when I knew that I could earn as much in a day by smearing my face with a little paint, laying my cap on the ground, and sitting still. It was a long fight between my pride and the money, but the dollars won at last, and I threw up reporting and sat day after day in the corner which I had first chosen, inspiring pity by my ghastly face and filling my pockets with coppers.[89] Only one man knew my secret. He was the keeper of a low den in which I used to lodge in Swandam Lane, where I could every morning emerge as a squalid beggar and in the evenings transform myself into a well-dressed man about town. This fellow, a Lascar, was well paid by me for his rooms, so that I knew that my secret was safe in his possession.

"Well, very soon I found that I was saving considerable sums of money. I do not mean that any beggar in the streets of London could earn £700[90] a year – which is less than my average takings – but I had exceptional advantages in my power of making up, and also in a facility of repartee,[91] which improved by practice and made me quite a recognized character in the City. All day a stream of pennies, varied by silver, poured in upon me, and it was a very bad day in which I failed to take £2.

"As I grew richer I grew more ambitious, took a house in the country, and eventually married, without anyone having a suspicion as to my real occupation. My dear wife knew that I had business in the City. She little knew what.

89 A one-penny coin. So-called as it was copper coloured.
90 A considerable wage: at the time a well-paid butler might earn £100 a year.
91 Witty banter.

"Last Monday I had finished for the day and was dressing in my room above the opium den when I looked out of my window and saw, to my horror and astonishment, that my wife was standing in the street, with her eyes fixed full upon me. I gave a cry of surprise, threw up my arms to cover my face, and, rushing to my confidant, the Lascar, entreated him to prevent anyone from coming up to me. I heard her voice downstairs, but I knew that she could not ascend. Swiftly I threw off my clothes, pulled on those of a beggar, and put on my pigments and wig. Even a wife's eyes could not pierce so complete a disguise. But then it occurred to me that there might be a search in the room, and that the clothes might betray me. I threw open the window, reopening by my violence a small cut which I had inflicted upon myself in the bedroom that morning. Then I seized my coat, which was weighted by the coppers which I had just transferred to it from the leather bag in which I carried my takings. I hurled it out of the window, and it disappeared into the Thames. The other clothes would have followed, but at that moment there was a rush of constables up the stair, and a few minutes after I found, rather, I confess, to my relief, that instead of being identified as Mr. Neville St. Clair, I was arrested as his murderer.

"I do not know that there is anything else for me to explain. I was determined to preserve my disguise as long as possible, and hence my preference for a dirty face. Knowing that my wife would be terribly anxious, I slipped off my ring and confided it to the Lascar at a moment when no constable was watching me, together with a hurried scrawl, telling her that she had no cause to fear."

"That note only reached her yesterday," said Holmes.

"Good God! What a week she must have spent!"

"The police have watched this Lascar," said Inspector Bradstreet, "and I can quite understand that he might find it difficult to post a letter unobserved. Probably he handed it to some sailor customer of his, who forgot all about it for some days."

"That was it," said Holmes, nodding approvingly; "I have no doubt of it. But have you never been prosecuted for begging?"

"Many times; but what was a fine to me?"

"It must stop here, however," said Bradstreet. "If the police are to hush this thing up, there must be no more of Hugh Boone."

"I have sworn it by the most solemn oaths which a man can take."

"In that case I think that it is probable that no further steps may be taken. But if you are found again, then all must come out. I am sure, Mr. Holmes, that we are very much indebted to you for having cleared the matter up. I wish I knew how you reach your results."

"I reached this one," said my friend, "by sitting upon five pillows and consuming an ounce of shag. I think, Watson, that if we drive to Baker Street we shall just be in time for breakfast."

ARTHUR CONAN DOYLE

Printed in Great Britain
by Amazon

37295125R00026